THE UNDER DOGS

ROCK'N'ROLL OVER

RAZORBILL

An imprint of
Penguin Random House LLC, New York

For Seb & Remy, rock on! —KT & JT

To all the cartoon
dogs I've loved before —SG

First published in Australia by Hardie Grant Children's Publishing in 2022
Published in the United States of America by Razorbill,
an imprint of Penguin Random House LLC, 2023
Text copyright © 2022 by Kate and Jol Temple
Illustration copyright © 2022 by Shiloh Gordon
Activities text copyright © 2023 by Penguin Random House LLC

Library of Congress Cataloging-in-Publication Data
Names: Temple, Kate, author. | Temple, Jol, author. |
Gordon, Shiloh, illustrator.
Title: Rock 'n' roll over / Kate and Jol Temple ; art by
Shiloh Gordon. Other titles: Rock and roll over
Description: New York : Razorbill, 2023. | Series:
The Underdogs | Audience: Ages 6-9 years. |
Summary: The Underdogs have a bone to pick with
whoever took a one-of-a-kind guitar.
Identifiers: LCCN 2022051258 (print) | LCCN
2022051259 (ebook) | ISBN 9780593527023 (trade
paperback) | ISBN 9780593527030 (epub)
Subjects: CYAC: Dogs–Fiction. | Cats–Fiction. | Mystery
and detective stories. | Humorous stories. | LCGFT:
Detective and mystery fiction. | Humorous fiction.
Classification: LCC PZ7.T246 Ro 2023 (print) |
LCC PZ7.T246 (ebook) | DDC [Fic]–dc23
LC record available at https://lccn.loc.gov/2022051258
LC ebook record available at
https://lccn.loc.gov/2022051259
Printed in the United States of America
1st Printing

Series design by Sarah Mitchell

LSCH

KATE AND JOL TEMPLE

The UNDER DOGS

ROCK'N'ROLL OVER

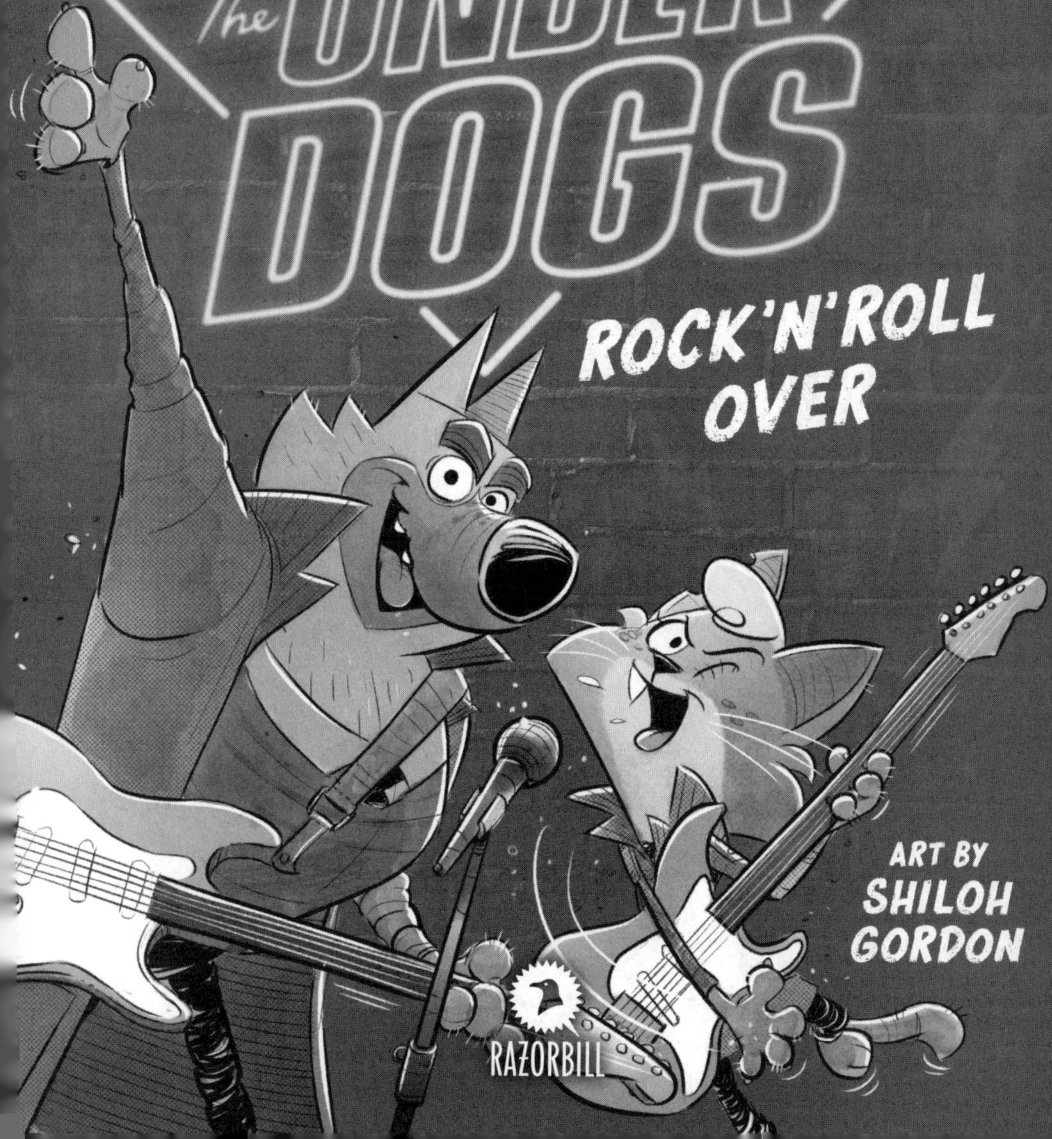

ART BY SHILOH GORDON

RAZORBILL

Hello, detective friends, we meet **again**. We're in the **headquarters** of the Underdog Detective Agency. You know the place. It's right above Mrs. McTavish's soup factory—the **stinky** heart of Dogtown.

What flavor is she cooking today?

I'm going to say . . . asparagus and lobster heads.

Today in the office there are not just **bad smells**, there are also **terrible sounds**!

Yep. That's Detective Barkley playing a trumpet. You see, the Underdogs are having a **slow day**. In fact, they've been having **A LOT** of slow days.

It seems that no matter **what** they do, they just don't get many **cases**. And what do dog detectives do when there are no mysteries to solve? They tidy up the office. That's what Barkley had been doing...at least, until he found his old **trumpet**.

"You played in a band?" asked Carl. "Me too!" He'd found a pair of **bongo drums** and was **bashing** away at them.

"You were a bongo doggo? **PAWSOME!**" said Barkley.

"Hey, Spots, look—I found your old **triangle**!" said Carl.

"You played the triangle?" Fang asked.

"Professionally!" said Barkley. "Before Spots was an Underdog, she played triangle in the **Dogtown Orchestra**!"

Spots laid down some **notes**.

"What about you, Fang? Did you ever play an **instrument**?" asked Spots.

Fang's fur **bristled** and she shook her head. "I was in the school band when I was a **kitten**, but that didn't work out."

"Forget about that! You should give it **another try**, Fang!" Carl offered her his set of bongo drums.

No, thanks. Playing music is not for me.

"Speaking of music," Barkley said. "Isn't there a big **concert** in Dogtown today?"

"DogAid!" yelped Carl. "It's going to be the **greatest** concert of all time!"

"Who's playing?" asked Barkley.

"Only all the **best artists** in the world!" yelped Carl. "The Rolling Bones, Barkoncé, the RaBones."

"You're forgetting the **cat** artists, Carl," added Fang. "Metallicat, Feline Dion, Snoop Catt."

"Never heard of any of them," said Barkley as he looked through his old **record collection**. "I'm a **jazz** dog through and through. Give me some Charlie Barker or Count Basset any day over your **rock stars**!"

Carl couldn't believe it. "What about Justin Beaver? The Mice Girls? Or Catty Perry? Or Lady BaaBaa? She's the **sheep** with those **wild hats**!"

But Barkley just shook his head. "That sounds like the **last** concert I'd ever want to go to," said Barkley. Clearly, he was **not impressed**.

"It's the **greatest** lineup of musicians Dogtown has **ever** seen!" said Dr. Spots, looking up from an invention she was tinkering with. "Besides, it's a **charity** concert, Barkley. Every ticket sold raises money to **help** stray dogs."

"Hmm, that is a good cause, Spots," Barkley admitted. "But no, thank you! I'll make a **donation** instead. You **won't** catch me at a rock 'n' roll show!"

Just then, the phone **rang**.

"**AAAAAARGH!**" cried Carl.

"It's just the phone. It does that," said Barkley, **shaking** his head.

Barkley picked up the phone. "Hello, this is the Underdog Detective Agency. How may I help you today? What? Our **limo** is outside? I think you've got the **wrong number**. We didn't order a limo."

But it **wasn't** a wrong number. The voice on the other end of the line wanted to talk to the Underdogs. And sure enough, Fang looked out the **window** and there **WAS** a limo waiting outside.

CHAPTER 2

Barkley and the Underdogs left the office. They took the **rickety** stairs down through Mrs. McTavish's Soup Factory and walked out to the street where the **limo** was parked.

The window on the limo rolled down just a **smidge**, and a dog's shiny **wet nose** poked out.

"Are you the Underdogs?" said a low voice.

"We are indeed!" said Fang.

"That's **confusing**, seeing as you're a **cat**," said the nose.

"Fang's one of our **best** detectives," barked Barkley. "Now who, may I ask, are you?"

The nose sniffed. "I represent a Very Important Pooch. For **privacy** reasons, I'd rather not **reveal** their name or mine right now."

So how can we help you?

I need you to track down a missing item.

"That's a **specialty** of ours! So what's missing?"

"For **privacy** reasons, I'd rather not say."

"You want us to track down **something** for **somebody** but we don't know who and we don't know what?" Barkley said, **stumped**.

I love a challenge!

"I never thought I'd say it, but **maybe** you should talk to the Top Dog Detectives instead," said Barkley.

The Top Dogs, of course, are the Underdogs' **archrivals**. The show-off brother and sister Weimaraners had heaps of **cool** detective vehicles and their own reality TV show.

TOP DOGS

NEW SERIES
FRIDAY 7PM

The nose **sniffed** again. "It seems the Top Dogs are too busy at the moment. They're preparing some **songs** to play at DogAid."

"The Top Dogs are playing at DogAid?!" yelped Carl. "Those dogs are the **best**!"

"Let's not get carried away, Carl," said Barkley, **shooting** him a look. "And Ms. Nose, don't you get carried away, either. There's nothing we can do if you can't give us any **information**."

The nose **twitched**. "I'm sorry, Underdogs. For privacy reasons, I'd rather not say." With that, the **wet**, **shiny** nose popped back inside the car, and the limo began to drive away.

"At least give us a **phone number** we can reach you on!" pleaded Barkley.

"How **mysterious**," said Fang as they went back to the office. "That's left me really scratching my head!"

"You should use flea shampoo," said Spots.

"No time for that now, Spots!" said Fang, still scratching. "Can you run a check on that **license plate**?"

"Sure can! I've actually designed an **app** for that!" said Spots as she typed the limo's number plate into her phone.

"Nice one, Spots," said Barkley.

"And I've got an app that can put a **bird beak** filter on your photos!"

"It seems the limo belongs to … Oh my dog!" said Spots. "You **won't** believe it! It's **MICK WAGGER**."

Fang and Carl **gasped**.

MICK WAGGER?

The famous lead singer of the Rolling Bones?

"Is he some sort of **rock star**?" asked Barkley.

"Mick Wagger is the biggest rock star of **all time**!" said Fang.

"And the **best** guitarist of all time too!" added Carl, rocking out with a ping-pong paddle.

DOGAID

"Mick Wagger must be in town for **DogAid**. We need to track him down!" Barkley said.

Barkley may not know much about rock 'n' roll, but he **sure** knows how to follow a clue.

"I'd bet one of my nine lives," said Fang, "that Mick Wagger is staying at the Howlton Hotel! That's where all the **Very Important Pooches** love to stay!"

"We'll take the Underdog **tricycle**!" shouted Fang as she made her way to the door.

"Umm … about that," said Barkley. "We sort of had to **sell** the tricycle. Times are tough, you know."

"Not again! So how are we meant to get **across town**?" grumbled Fang.

"I think I can help," said Spots. "Let me reveal my latest and **greatest** invention."

Spots held up a pair of shoes that looked **exactly** like rollerblades.

"They look like shoes, right? Wrong! They have **wheels**!"

"They're **rollerblades**," said Fang flatly.

"Rollerblades? Now that's a **GREAT** name! Because look! They roll!" said Spots, spinning the wheels with her paw. "I was going to call them **Wheel Shoes**."

"Um…" said Fang. "They've **already** been invented, Spots. You can buy them at K9Mart."

But Spots **wasn't** listening.

"This line of little wheels means that when you put them on your feet, you can **zip** along at great speed! Cool, right?" said Spots.

"Yeah, cool, Spots. Already invented, but really cool," Barkley said, **shaking** his head.

Fang and Barkley each **slipped** on a pair of rollerblades and gave them a go.

"What's this **button** here do?" asked Fang, pointing to a **flashing** red button.

"Oh, don't touch that! It's a **turbo booster**. I've been **tinkering** with it, but I haven't ironed out all the kinks. So, for now, just get **rolling**!" said Spots.

Fang **zipped** across the office floor, getting the hang of the blades. "These could work," she said. But Barkley wasn't quite as **graceful** as Fang. Dogs often aren't.

SPLAT!

Poor Barkley. I'm sure he'll get the hang of them **soon**.

Hmm. **Maybe not.**

CHAPTER 3

Barkley and Fang **clattered** their way down the stairs and on to the street. Fang glided her way across town and Barkley **banged** dangerously from lamppost to lamppost. Eventually they made it to the **fancy-pants** Howlton Hotel.

Fang walked up to the reception desk. "Would you please let Mr. Wagger know that the Underdogs are here to see him."

The kelpie at the front desk **laughed** out loud. Then she pointed to a **line** of fans, all dressed in Rolling Bones T-shirts and holding signs. "You can wait over there and maybe catch a **glimpse** of him like all the other Boneheads."

"Boneheads is what Rolling Bones **fans** call themselves, Barkley," explained Fang.

"Oh. I see," said Barkley, looking at the crowd of Boneheads all **eagerly** waiting outside the hotel.

Fang scanned the room, looking for another way to get upstairs, and **BINGO!** She spotted one.

"That might get us upstairs," said Fang, **pointing** to a sign in the lobby.

Barkley looked over. Next to the **sign** was a table where a friendly Labrador was handing out **lanyards**.

Fang quickly **glanced** down at the lanyards on the desk.

"Good day. We are Mr. Rex and Mr. Rover. I see you have our lanyards waiting for us," said Fang, pointing to **two name tags**.

"Mr. Rex?" said the slightly confused Labrador. "I was expecting you to be a dog, Mr. Rex, with a name like that. Are you **sure** you're here for the violin conference?" he asked.

ANNUAL
VIOLIN-
MAKERS
CONFERENCE
MR. REX

A quick-thinking Fang **grabbed** a violin on the table and **plucked** a string.

"Hmm, that's out of tune," said Fang, **twisting** the pegs. "There, that's better," she said, handing back the instrument.

Barkley raised his eyebrows in **surprise**.

"My apologies—here's your lanyard, Mr. Rex. Have a **wonderful** day at the conference!"

Fang and Barkley made their way to the **elevators**. "I'll bet another of my nine lives that Mick Wagger will have hired out the **entire** top floor just for himself. He's such a rock star," said Fang as she waited for the elevator to arrive.

The elevator doors opened. And who do you think was inside? Yep, Mick Wagger. Out he **pranced**, an energetic border collie in big sunglasses and leopard-print pants. He sure was one **cool-looking** canine.

What's up, dog? And cat? Ooh! Nice lanyards.

MICK WAGGER:
• Border collie
• World-famous rock star
• Wearer of snazzy pants

Fang went to speak ... but **nothing** came out. You see, Fang was a bit of a Bonehead herself. She loved the Rolling Bones and had listened to **ALL** their songs. Now here she was, standing in front of Mick Wagger, and, well, the cat had her **tongue**. Not literally! It just means she couldn't find the right words to say.

Barkley, on the other hand, had no idea who this **dancing** dog was. "Excuse me, are you going to step out of the elevator or just keep dancing?"

Before Fang could tell Barkley that this was the **famous** rock dog they wanted to talk to, the Boneheads had spotted Mick and were **rushing** over to get an autograph.

"**EEEK!**" shrieked Mick.

Just before they were all **squashed** by the **stampede** of Boneheads, the elevator doors shut and the elevator started to **climb**.

"Whew! That was a close one!" said Mick, catching his breath. "I guess you want an autograph too?" said Mick, handing Fang a **squiggly** signature.

Fang popped the autograph in her **pocket** before finding her **voice**. "Um … Mr. Wagger, actually, I'm not after an autograph … We're the Underdogs."

Mick took another look at their lanyards. "No, you're not. You're Mr. Rover. And you're Mr. Rex … aren't you?"

"Just a **clever** disguise," said Fang.

We're here to help you, Mr. Wagger. We've heard that you might need a couple of detectives.

Just then Mick hit the big red **EMERGENCY** button that **stopped** the elevator in its tracks.

"We know you need our help," said Barkley. Mick nodded and spoke in a **hushed** voice.

"Can you keep a secret?" asked Mick.

"Of course, we are professional detectives," replied Fang.

"OK then…" whimpered Mick. "My **golden guitar** is **missing**!"

"Your guitar?" said Fang.

Without it, I'll be ruined!

Fang and Barkley looked at each other, then at Mick. "Um... sorry to hear that, Mr. Wagger. But can't you just play **another** guitar?"

"Of course I've got spare guitars. **Thousands** of them. But only one **Isabella**."

"Isabella? Who's Isabella?" asked Barkley.

"Isabella is my guitar! My **lucky** guitar. I never go onstage without her. I can't play without her. You mustn't breathe a word of this to **anybody**!"

Barkley and Fang **nodded**.

Mick pressed the button, sending the elevator up.
The doors opened right onto the **penthouse apartment**.
It was **luxury** like Fang and Barkley had never seen
before. Marble floors, a **giant** clamshell dog bath, even
a Puplo Picasso painting hanging on the wall!

48

And there, in a **plush** leather chair, sat a Cavalier King Charles spaniel in a suit. Her nose looked very **familiar**.

"You're Ms. Nose!" barked Barkley, looking at the Cavalier's wet, shiny **nose**.

"You don't have to be so **secretive**, Louise," said Mick. "This is Mr. Rex and Mr. Rover of the Underdogs. I've just told them all about Isabella."

The Cavalier smiled. "I'm Louise. I'm Mick's **manager**, and I'm pleased to see you followed the clues all the way here. Looks like you are the **right** detectives for the case after all."

The Underdogs are the right detectives for any case. No clue left undug.

Louise took a **slurp** of tea from her teacup. "Care for a cup of tea? We have Dog's Breakfast or Earl Greyhound."

"No, thank you. We'll just ask a few **questions** and then be on our way," Barkley said, taking out his **notebook**.

Do you know anyone who would want to steal your lucky guitar?

Mick looked at Fang. "It could be **ANYONE!** Boneheads love collecting anything to do with me. Wait! You don't think one of my **fans** would have stolen it, do you?"

"At this stage, everyone's a **suspect**," said Barkley.

"Excuse me, Mr. Wagger," said Fang. "You said you can't play without your lucky guitar. Why is that?"

"I get so nervous. I just **freeze!**" shrieked Mick Wagger.

Fang thought about that for a **moment** before turning her one eye toward Louise. "Is there anybody who'd want to see Mick put on a **bad** show at DogAid?"

Barkley smiled. This was good detective thinking. Fang was a **real** Underdog.

Louise hesitated before answering. "Mick is known for his **big** mouth."

"Whaaaat?" Mick acted **surprised**.

MEEEEEE?

Mick looked a little **sheepish**, which is not to say he looked like a sheep at all, just a little **embarrassed**. He still looked like a sheepdog, which is after all a job that a lot of border collies have.

"I guess it's true. I do have a **big mouth**. It could almost be **anybody** who stole my guitar!" said Mick.

"Don't worry, Mr. Wagger. We'll **find** your golden guitar," said Barkley. "Now, how long do we have until you need it?"

"**Four hours**!" wailed Mick. "I'm due **onstage** right after that dancing fluffball, Lady BaaBaa."

Fang and Barkley looked at each other. Four hours wasn't long enough to dig up a **bone**, let alone find a missing guitar!

CHAPTER 4

Fang and Barkley took the **elevator** back down to the lobby.

"We don't have much time, and this missing guitar could be almost **anywhere**," said Barkley.

"That's true, but right now every musician in Dogtown is **busy** getting ready for DogAid. If we're looking for a missing guitar, we need to go to the **Dogtown Arena** and have a look around," said Fang.

Just before Barkley could say, what a great idea, the elevator doors opened. In stepped a **sleek-looking** cat holding something in her paws. A **guitar case**! Fang was starstruck; this wasn't any old cat.

CATTY PERRY:
- World-famous pop singer
- Very fashionable cat

Oh wow! You're Catty Perry! I love your music!

Thanks. I love your lanyards.

Fang had been a **fan** of Catty's since she was a **kitten**, and she couldn't ever remember her playing the guitar.

Catty looked a little uncomfortable. She **clutched** the guitar case **closer** to herself. "Just trying out a new sound."

The elevator doors opened and she **rushed** out into the lobby.

"I wonder what's up with that cat," said Barkley. "She sure looked **jittery** when you mentioned that guitar case. Could it be the missing guitar?"

"No way! I'm sure Catty Perry wouldn't **steal** a guitar..." said Fang.

By the time the two of them had **slipped** their rollerblades on, Catty was long gone. They decided to **skate** across town anyway, and made their way to Dogtown Arena. Barkley was doing a little better on the rollerblades now. They **zipped** by the post office and the second-paw bookshop filled with dog-eared books. As they **rolled** by Sunglass Kennel, a **question** popped into Barkley's head.

"How did you know how to **tune** that violin, Fang?" asked Barkley cautiously. "I thought you said **playing music** wasn't for you."

"It isn't!" **snapped** Fang. She kept on rolling.

Barkley didn't want to upset Fang, so he dropped it. But, being a detective, Barkley was still **curious** to know. Maybe Fang would tell him another time. Maybe.

Anyhow, they soon arrived at Dogtown Arena and **skated** right on in. The place was **buzzing** with dogs setting up for the afternoon's big concert. Muscly pitbulls and Staffordshires lugged heavy **equipment** around. They **unloaded** big trucks and rigged up lights and loudspeakers on the main stage. Small dogs were **scampering** up scaffolding and **barking** over walkie-talkies.

A stressed-out Pekingese wearing a **headset** ran by with a **clipboard** but stopped in her tracks when she saw the Underdogs.

She looked him **up** and **down**.

"We're the Underdogs," explained Fang. The Pekingese looked at them **blankly**. It seemed she'd never heard of the Underdogs before.

"We're detectives," Fang went on. "We're **investigating** a case."

"Really? What kind of case? A **guitar** case? A **tuba** case? A **keyboard** case? They're all here," said the Pekingese, pointing to a **sea** of musical instrument cases.

Finding the guitar here would be like looking for a needle in a haystack!

"Why would anybody look for a **needle** in a **haystack**?" Fang asked, confused. "I'd always check the sewing kit first. A haystack would be the **last** place you'd ever find a needle."

I don't have time for this!

Sorry. Do you mind if we take a look around?

"Just don't get in the way!" said the **bossy** Pekingese. "And if you see those toilet guys, tell them I'm looking for them. We've got a **hundred thousand** rock fans here today and not so much as a **single** tree to whiz on!"

With the Pekingese gone, Fang and Barkley were free to **sniff** out clues.

"I think we need to start **interviewing** suspects," said Barkley.

"Did someone say interview?" squawked a **fancy-looking** canary. It was none other than the famous singer Mariah Canary.

MARIAH CANARY:
- World's most famous canary
- Powerful singing voice
- Not so fond of cats

"We'd love to ask you a few **questions**, Mariah Canary," said Fang.

The canary looked Fang up and down and put her **beak** in the air.

"On second thought, no thanks. I don't talk to cats." With that, Mariah **waddled** away.

Lucky for the Underdogs, a dog in a **leather jacket** was coming their way, and she was holding a guitar case. Fang knew **exactly** who it was. It was Billie Irish-Setter—the famous rock singer.

BILLIE IRISH-SETTER

- Famous rock singer
- Likes changing her fur color
- Youngest award-winning rock star in history

Barkley had **no idea** who she was, but he took out his pencil and notepad anyway.

"Do you know Mick Wagger?" Barkley asked.

Billie **scoffed**. "He said I couldn't **clap**! But I'm going to show him," said Billie. Barkley's ears pricked up.

It was at this point that two **burly** Rottweilers appeared next to Fang and Barkley. Security dogs.

They didn't **waste** any time **tossing** Fang and Barkley back out onto the street.

CHAPTER 5

Now that Fang and Barkley had been **tossed** out of Dogtown Arena, they couldn't even look for clues! Maybe they should just **pack up** for the day, head home and do whatever Underdogs do when they're **not** solving crimes. But is that what you would do? Of course not! **YOU** would want to solve the mystery. **YOU** would want to find the guitar thief! And that's exactly how Fang and Barkley felt too! Because Underdogs **never** give up. No clue left undug! What they needed was a **fresh** plan and a **new** idea, and luckily, that's exactly what Fang had in mind.

"I've got an **idea**! I know how we can get back in," said Fang. "But we're going to need some **disguises**."

"Great thinking, Fang! If we dress up as rock stars, **nobody** will know it's us!"

This wasn't what Fang was thinking at all, but she did have a little **giggle** when she **imagined** Barkley dressing up as a rock star like David Bow-Wow or Fido Mercury.

"Actually, Barkley, I've got a **better** idea. I was thinking we could disguise ourselves as **toilet installers**."

Barkley looked **confused**.

That Pekingese said they need toilets and those toilet installers haven't arrived yet!

75

Barkley thought about it for a second. "It **could** work! And no one will pay any **attention** to a couple of toilet installers."

"Exactly," said Fang as Barkley **bumped** her paw.

Let me call Carl and get him to find us some **GREAT** disguises!

Back at Underdogs **headquarters**, Carl was **staring** at the **ringing** phone.

Spots shook her head, then **leaned** over and answered it.

Oh, hello, Barkley. How's the investigation going?

It's going great, Spots! I think we've got a couple of leads, but we're going to need to go undercover and we don't have much time.

Spots looked over at the **huge** wardrobe of disguises. "What do you want to be? A drummer? A security dog? A singing cowboy? You name it, we've got it."

"We need some toilet-installer disguises!"

There was **silence** on the phone.

"That's pretty random," said Spots, **scratching** her spots. "But you can count on us! We'll get our rollerblades on and bring them over **faster** than a greyhound in a sports car!"

After Barkley hung up, the two Underdogs hid in the bushes, **waiting** for the disguises and **watching** all the activity at the arena. There was a lot to see; some fans were beginning to turn up, forming long lines at the gate, while **limos** kept dropping off rock stars. It sure was going to be hard to find out who took the **golden guitar**.

"Almost anyone here could have stolen Mick's guitar," said Barkley. "Those **five mice** look **very** suspicious."

"They're the Mice Girls," said Fang.

"What about the **beaver**? I don't trust him," said Barkley.

"**NO WAY!** That's Justin Beaver."

"Hmm. There's that canary again."

"Mariah Canary? She was a bit **cagey**."

"What about that **fluffy goat** there?"

"That's no goat. That's a sheep! Lady BaaBaa!" Fang **yelped** excitedly.

I literally don't know any of these singers . . .

"Lady BaaBaa? She's the best! You should see her **outfits** and her **amazing** hats!"

Fang got out her mobile phone and showed Barkley a few shots of Lady BaaBaa in her **outrageous** outfits. In one shot she was wearing a dress made completely out of **liver treats** and wearing a hat made out of a giant chew toy. The whole of Dogtown had gone **wild** over that outfit!

LADY BAABAA:
- World's most famous sheep
- Great singer and dancer
- Amazing outfits

"Whoa!" said Barkley. "A real **master** of disguise!"

"It's true." Fang **chuckled**. "She could be an Underdog if she wasn't already a rock star!"

Just then Barkley and Fang heard a **banging** sound coming from a nearby recycling bin. Then a really **weird** thing happened. The bin started **talking**.

"Pssst!" said the bin. "You two! Over here!"

"Hmm. That **bin** is trying to get our attention," said Barkley.

"Wow, Dogtown really takes **recycling** seriously," said Fang.

"It's us!" Out of the top of the bin **poked** Carl and Spots.

Fang smiled in **surprise**. "Great disguise, guys!"

This is nothing. Wait until you see the disguises we got for you!

Barkley was **excited**. These toilet-installer disguises would be their ticket back into the music festival.

After a bit of **shuffling** around inside the bush, Carl pulled out something they **weren't** expecting.

"What are these toilets for?" said Barkley, making a **face**.

"They're not toilets. They're toilet disguises! Just like you **asked** for!" said Spots proudly.

Fang and Barkley **groaned**.

"Not **toilet** disguises. **TOILET-INSTALLER** disguises!"

That makes more sense!

I thought it was a weird request.

"What are we going to do with these!" shrieked Barkley.

"They're the latest **technology**," said Spots. "I even managed to put an emergency button on the flush, so if you get in **trouble**, we can find you—all you have to do is **flush**!"

"That"s very **clever**, Spots," said Barkley. "But we can't dress up as toilets and **walk** around!"

Fang looked at Barkley. Barkley looked at Fang.
Fang looked back at Barkley.

"Maybe we can?" said Fang, slipping on one of the
toilet suits. "It's the **pawfect** disguise."

Barkley knew Fang was right. No one would **suspect**
a toilet. So, with time **ticking** before the concert was
due to begin, Barkley swallowed his pride. *GULP!*
And **jumped** into the toilet.

CHAPTER 6

Barkley and Fang **quietly** approached the gate. From where they were hiding, Barkley could see that the security dogs had already posted up **pictures** of Fang and Barkley to stop them from getting in.

"I don't like our chances," whispered Barkley.

"Just act **casual**," Fang said.

"How does a toilet act casual?" grumbled Barkley.

Now, if you've ever tried to **sneak** into a music festival (or anywhere!) dressed as a toilet, then you'll know that it's not that easy. When the security guards weren't looking, the Underdog toilets **crept** closer to the gate. But as the guards turned back, the Underdog toilets **froze** in their tracks.

"Hey, who put a couple of **toilets** here?" said one of the security guards, looking at the toilets that had **suddenly** appeared out of nowhere. Fang peered out through the lid.

"Hey, is there **someone** in that toilet?" said one security guard.

"No," said the toilet.

The security guards looked at each other. This was **very** suspicious. But just when it looked like the game was up, the Underdogs had a stroke of **luck** in the shape of a **stressed-out** Pekingese.

"My toilets!" yelled the Pekingese from the **main stage**. "Can someone bring them over here?"

And with that, Fang and Barkley ran as **fast** as they could, past the suspicious security guards and through the open gate.

"Wow, they can **walk** too! They really **ARE** high-tech toilets," said the security guard.

The Underdogs were back inside the **festival** and things were even **busier** than before. Fang could see some of the musicians doing their sound checks. A bunch of **food trucks** were setting up to keep the crowd fed. Look! Even Mrs. McTavish was pulling up in her soup van. I sure hope people like her turnip and squid soup! **YUCK!** There was a sea of **equipment** and carts over by the main stage.

"We better **hurry**. The concert is starting in an **hour**!"
said Fang.

"Then it's time to track down **clues**!" barked Barkley.
"And I want to get a look at Billie Irish-Setter's guitar.
Where should we begin?"

"Backstage!" said Fang. "That's where the rock stars
hang out!" The two of them **shuffled** across the
grounds. "Toilets coming through!"

They **waddled** up a set of stairs that led to the backstage area. This was the space reserved just for the rock stars. There were **comfy** couches to relax on, a fridge where you could help yourself to a bottle of 7 Pup or a can of Dr. Pupper, and bowls full of tasty **treats** to snack on. A few of the rock stars were already tuning their **instruments** and getting ready for the big show to start.

One of the **musicians**—a beaver with an acoustic guitar—looked up as the toilets entered.

"Oh, **FINALLY!** We've got toilets! Thank dog for that!" said Justin Beaver. He was **busting**!

Barkley had to think fast. He **popped** up out of the toilet.

Uh, sorry. We are not toilets. We are **THE TOILETS**. The band. Of course you've heard of us, we're very famous.

Justin Beaver went **red** in the face. He didn't want to let on that he'd never heard of the band the Toilets, not in front of all the other rock stars. So, instead of telling the **truth**, he said, "Of course! The Toilets! I **LOVE** your music!"

And once Justin Beaver had said he **liked** their music, well, that was enough for all the other musicians to say the **same** thing.

Oh wow! The Toilets. You guys are amazing.

Your first album was, like, so inspirational.

It's so cool that the Toilets are at DogAid too!

While Barkley was **pretending** to be a famous toilet, Fang helped herself to some of the **yummy** snacks. Yep, she could get used to this rockstar life. But they weren't here for the **snacks**—they needed in-**FUR**-mation!

"Mind if we have a look at your guitars?" asked Barkley, heading over to a row of guitars in the corner. They were **nice-looking** guitars, but none of them were the **golden** guitar Mick Wagger called Isabella.

Just then, a fluffy white cloud **floated** in. "What **AMAAAAAAAAAAAZING** costumes!" it said.

Barkley looked up. The fluffy white **cloud** was actually that fluffy white **sheep**. A fluffy white sheep in high heels, a ballet tutu, and the most **outrageous** hat Barkley had ever seen!

"**LADY BAABAA?**" said Barkley.

"The one and **only**, darling," said the **stylish** sheep. "You must give me the name of your fashion designer. Those toilet suits are **absolutely** divine!"

"Why, thank you," said Barkley. "They do make quite the **splash**, don't they?"

The big **fluffball** turned and **stomped** off toward her dressing room.

"Wow!" said Fang. "This concert is going to be the **best**!"

"Maybe," said Barkley. "But only if we can find Mick Wagger's **missing** guitar."

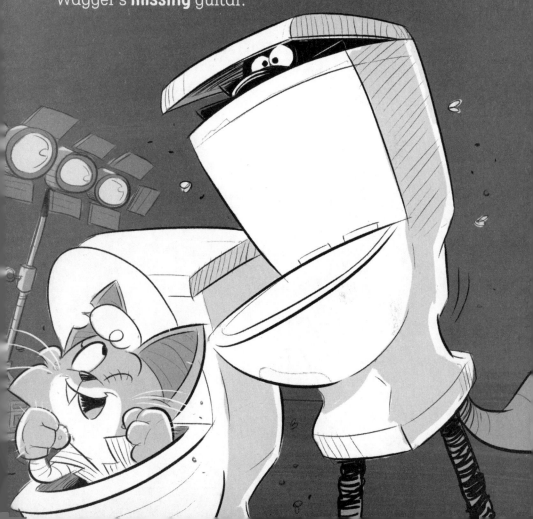

CHAPTER 7

With the concert set to start in **less** than an hour, the Underdogs sure had their work cut out for them. After **snooping** around in the backstage lounge without any luck, it was time to go and **sniff** around the equipment they'd seen on their way in.

Fang and Barkley had seen a lot of **instrument** cases in the **loading area**, so they decided to head out there and have a look. Now, you might think it's a bit **weird** to see a couple of toilets **poking** around the loading bay...

But, actually, it was a **very** good cover.

Fang and Barkley worked their way through **every** guitar case, **every** bass guitar case, **every** keyboard case. One after another. There sure were a lot of them! When Fang finally got to the very **last** case, she took a deep **breath**, hoping it would contain the golden guitar.

No such luck.

"We must have opened every guitar case in Dogtown!" said Fang, wiping **sweat** from her fur.

"Not **every** guitar case," said Barkley as a **flashy** yellow sports car pulled into the loading bay. You guessed it. It was Catty Perry.

"Hide!" hissed Fang. Barkley and Fang **jumped** behind the pile of instrument cases.

"Is she **playing** in the concert too?" whispered Barkley.

"Well, she's not here for Mrs. McTavish's soup," replied Fang as they **watched** her step out of the sports car.

Good day, Catty.

Catty Perry didn't know that the Underdogs were watching her every **move**. But when she opened the boot of her car, the Underdogs saw her. And when she pulled out a guitar case and looked around **suspiciously**, the Underdogs were **right** there to see that too.

But Fang was **already** on her tail. Cats know when cats are up to something, and Fang was right about Catty—she was definitely behaving **strangely**.

Catty made her way up from the loading bay to the backstage area, and every time she walked past someone, Fang noticed that Catty hid the guitar case **behind** her. The Underdogs **trailed** her to the rock stars' lounge, but she didn't go inside. Instead, she looked around to see if anyone was nearby, and then she slipped behind the **backstage** curtain.

MAIN STAGE

The Underdogs **dashed** over to the curtain.

"The game's up, Ms. Perry. It's time to **hand over** that guitar," said Barkley. But when they pulled back the curtain, there was **no one** on the other side.

"Look, Barkley, Catty left it behind!" said Fang, holding up the case.

"**THE GUITAR CASE!**" said Barkley.

"And not **ANY** guitar case. I'd recognise that **squiggle** anywhere. This is Mick Wagger's autograph!" said Fang, opening the case up.

Barkley and Fang **stared** at the violin. This was the right guitar case for sure, but this was **not** the right guitar. It wasn't a guitar at all. It was a **violin**. Fang **shuddered**.

"What's Catty Perry doing with a violin? She **doesn't** play **violin**," Fang said.

"And what's she doing with Mick Wagger's guitar case? She's probably **swapped** the guitar out for this violin. And if that's true, that means..."

"We need to find that cat—and fast, **very fast**," said Barkley, and he was right. Because right at that moment, a **limousine** was pulling up at DogAid and inside it was a very **nervous** Mick Wagger.

CHAPTER 8

Fang and Barkley **grabbed** the case with the violin in it
and **ran** out to meet the limousine. The window **rolled**
down and out **popped** a nose.

"Is Mick in there with you?" said Barkley.

"For **privacy** reasons, I'd rather not say," said Louise.

"We need to talk to him," said Fang.

"Mick doesn't talk to **toilets**," said Louise.

"It's us! The Underdogs," said Barkley.

"Oh, my **mistake**. I thought you were toilets," said Louise, rolling the window down a **little** more. Just at that moment, a very nervous Mick Wagger **peered** over Louise's shoulder.

"Did you find my golden guitar? Please tell me you **found** it!" shrieked Mick.

Barkley straightened up and tried to look **serious**, which is very **hard** to do when you're in a toilet.

"Mr. Wagger, can you **identify** this guitar case?" said Barkley, holding up the case. Mick Wagger's eyes lit up and he **flung** open the limousine door.

"**MY ISABELLA!**" shrieked the rock star. He threw open the case, only to find the violin. "You've ... **shrunk**?!"

"About that," said Fang. "We haven't found your guitar, but we are **very** close."

Then the Pekingese with the **clipboard** appeared.

"Oh, Mr. Wagger, thank dogness, you've arrived! I've been looking for you. You're on in **thirty minutes**."

"But I **don't** have my guitar!" squealed Mick Wagger.

"Oh, don't **worry**, Mr. Wagger, I'm sure we can find you one," said the Pekingese as she pushed the **hysterical** rock star toward the backstage lounge.

"*FIND MY GUITAR, UNDERDOGS!*" shrieked Mick Wagger as he disappeared up the stairs.

"You **heard** him, Underdogs," said Louise. "If you don't get him that guitar, his career will be **ruined**. And do you know what that means?"

Fang and Barkley **shook** their heads.

"You'll be ruined too. I'll personally see to it that you **never** get another case again. Then you'll **really** be in the toilet," snapped Louise.

With that, Louise **straightened** her suit and **dashed** off after Mick.

Barkley turned to Fang.

"She's right, if we don't **solve** this case we might not get another case again," said Barkley. "And you heard that Pekingese—we **only** have thirty minutes!"

"Wait," said Fang, turning on her tail. "If we need to speed things up, let's try out Spots's **rocket boosters**."

Fang and Barkley pulled on their rollerblades and pressed the **flashing** red buttons.

Nothing happened.

Oh well.

"I guess I didn't expect it to **WOOOOOOOOOOOOOORK!**"
screamed Barkley as he and Fang shot off like rockets.

Travelling at **breakneck** speed, the Underdogs **flew**
through the loading bay...

...past **backstage** and through the VIP area.

They narrowly missed **slamming** into various rock dogs **tuning** their instruments.

Barkley and Fang **zipped** out through the VIP gate and into the **audience**.

VIP AREA

Their eyes were **peeled** for Catty. The crowd had grown to a huge size, and creatures of all sorts **stamped** their feet and **clapped** their paws, waiting for the show to begin.

Then a big **BOOM** could be heard from the stage and golden glitter rained down on the **excited** audience. Fang and Barkley grabbed a nearby post to stop themselves in their tracks, and looked up at the stage.

There, among the **flashing** stage lights, was a big golden fluffball with the most amazing **hat** Fang had ever seen. Lady BaaBaa was right. She certainly was going to **STEAL** the show, because on top of that hat was the most **amazing** golden guitar.

"It's **not** a cat we should've been looking for," said Barkley. "It's a **sheep**!"

CHAPTER 9

Lady BaaBaa **strutted** onstage in her golden outfit. It sure was impressive. Her white fur had been **puffed** up and dyed a **sparkly** gold, she wore golden sneakers, and her giant guitar hat sparkled and **flickered** in the lights.

"Do you like my hat?!" said Lady BaaBaa from the stage. The crowd went **wild**. Dogs barked. Cats **meowed**. The few rabbits that were also there let out excited **squeaks**. Lady BaaBaa danced and sang, and with every dance move the guitar **teetered**, threatening to **tumble** off into the crowd.

Fang and Barkley **gasped**.

"We need to get that guitar before it ends up in the crowd!" said Fang.

"But how?" said Barkley. "She's onstage, we can't just **walk** onstage!"

"Maybe we **can**," said Fang.

"But only **performers** can go onstage," said Barkley.

"Exactly," said Fang.

"I'll hit the **emergency** flush button," said Barkley. "That will let Spots and Carl know to come and find us."

Barkley flushed his toilet suit, which sent a **signal** to Spots and Carl who were actually in the audience **dancing** to Lady BaaBaa.

Fang and Barkley let go of the pole they'd been **clinging** to, and, as soon as they did, they both went flying toward the stage on the **turbo** blades.

The Underdogs **flew** through the excited crowd. A burly security guard was just about to stop them heading backstage, but they were traveling too **fast**.

Barkley and Fang **switched** off their rollerblades and came to a sudden stop in the rockstar lounge, where Mick Wagger was trying out a **new** guitar. It wasn't pretty.

When Mick saw Barkley and Fang, a look of **desperation** crossed his face.

Tell me you found my guitar?! I'm on in five minutes!

We've found it all right.

TWANNNNGG-RURRRP!

Fang walked over to where Catty Perry was standing at the back of the room.

"I'm going to need to **borrow** your violin," said Fang.

Catty went **red** in the fur.

"I don't play the violin; I'm a **cool** cat," lied Catty. "Violins are for squares."

"There's nothing **wrong** with playing the violin," said Fang as she opened the guitar case and pulled out the violin. Then she put the violin to her chin and began to **play**.

NEWS FLASH! Fang was amazing! I don't mean a little bit amazing, I mean Fang was **superb**. She could *really* play that violin.

"You can **really** play!" Catty said.

At that moment, Spots and Carl appeared.

I didn't know Fang could play the violin!

Barkley couldn't believe his ears. Fang was **PAWSOME!** "Someone throw me a **trumpet**," he said. "It's time to get the **band** together!"

With that, Spots grabbed a **triangle** and Carl borrowed a pair of **drumsticks**, and the Underdogs headed toward the stage.

The Underdogs **climbed** the stairs to the edge of the stage. From there, they could see thousands of **excited** fans. Suddenly, Fang's fur **prickled**.

Fang felt her heart **banging**, but even though she was scared, she did a brave thing and **stepped** toward the stage. She was going to do this!

But two very **large** Rottweilers had other ideas.

"Onstage," said Fang. "We're the Toilets!"

Spots reached down and hit the **turbo boosters** on their rollerblades.

The Underdogs **zoomed** past the security guards and **burst** onstage. The crowd didn't know who the musicians dressed as toilets were, but they went **wild** for them anyway.

And when Fang let out one of her violin **solos**, they really **cheered!** Lady BaaBaa thought the cheering was for her, until Carl started a **drum** solo.

Then the crowd was cheering for **THE TOILETS!**

Lady BaaBaa **spun** around to see that the Underdogs were **stealing** the show. She was so **mad** that she took off her guitar hat and **threw** it into the air.

Quickly, Fang dropped her violin and **jumped** after the golden guitar, **catching** it just in time to save it from **smashing** into tiny bits and pieces!

With the **golden guitar** safely in Fang's **paws**, the Underdogs left the stage and headed back into the rockstar lounge. Fang could still hear the crowd **calling** for more.

TOILETS!

TOILETS!

Backstage, Mick Wagger was **pacing** the room anxiously. He **stopped** in his tracks when he saw Fang, who handed him the golden guitar. Mick Wagger let out a **cry**.

ISABELLA! My guitar! You found her! Where was she?

"I think Lady BaaBaa might be able to answer that," said Fang, turning to the **disheveled** golden singer–who was looking **quite** sheepish, even for a sheep.

"**YOU** took my guitar!" said Mick angrily.

"Well, you said I dance like a **goat**. And you're always such a show-off, so I thought I might steal the show for once. But I was **always** going to return it," said Lady BaaBaa weakly.

"We've got some **apologizing** to do too," said Fang, turning to Catty. "I'm **sorry** we thought you took the guitar," continued Fang.

Catty turned to Fang. "Forget about it," she said, kindly offering a **paw**. Fang took it and the two cats **shook** on it.

It's water off a cat's back!

"But tell me, Catty, **how** did you get the case? And **why** did you put a violin in it?"

Catty smiled. "I was at the Howlton Hotel for the violin-makers convention. You see, I've **always** wanted to play **classical** violin, but I was too embarrassed to tell anyone. So, I bought this violin and on my way out I found this **empty** guitar case."

With all those rock dogs in the hotel, I thought I would hide it in there.

Barkley **nodded**. "That makes sense. Looks like you were just a red herring."

"I'm a **cat**, not a fish!" said Catty.

"It's just a detective saying. It means you **weren't** the culprit. It was Lady BaaBaa all along," said Barkley. "I've got a **question** of my own. How did you learn to play the violin like that, Fang?"

"Thanks, Barkley," said Fang. "I used to **play** a lot. I was even in the Dogtown School Band." She paused.

"But one day I had a nasty **accident** and one of the violin strings **snapped** in the middle of a song," Fang said.

"Is that how you **lost** your eye?"

Fang nodded.

That's why I was so nervous about playing it onstage, I guess. But you know what? After today, I think that's going to change.

Lady BaaBaa **apologized** for taking Mick's guitar and Mick apologized for saying **mean** things.

Wool you forgive me, Mick?

Of course I will, BaaBaa!

And that's **nice**, but sometimes you need **actions** to make stuff right. So the sheepish sheep decided she was going to **auction** off all her fabulous hats and give the **money** to DogAid.

So Mick invited her onstage to do **just** that. The crowd went **WILD!** They even got an unexpected **duet** too!

The next day, every newspaper in Dogtown was saying it was the **best** concert that had ever happened. Rock 'n' roll history had been made and a rock 'n' roll **mystery** had been solved! There was even a **special** mention of that mysterious **band**—the Toilets!

So long, readers! Until next time we meet, when the Underdogs **crack** their next **case**!

THE END

DO **YOU** HAVE WHAT IT TAKES TO BE AN **UNDERDOG** DETECTIVE?

SEARCH & FIND

A good detective can find hidden evidence. Can you find these ten words in the below grid?

**CLIPBOARD   LIMO   KEYBOARD   COSTUME   GUITAR
HEADSET   AUDIENCE   SHEEP   GOLDEN   STRAY**

```
I N G V K P A C J W H W J A E
G T Z M Q L C V J S F Z U X C
V I E M X O Z R Y W Z W X J N
O O U S T Z Q N B S Q W P E
F P K T D L S T T K F R V T I
U U U U P A I W X E Z A G F D
L M A C K Y E M B Y F L M P U
E R A T I U G H O B T Y W N A
Z J O T B S I V M O Z L D P W
S P F W B A S D X A R Q E A O
N T C L I P B O A R D E K C U
Y X R A A H Q E U D H E R F X
V J N A L F R I L S X U D A D
F N M O Y A V J M P D B Y D J
W U G G O L D E N R O Q I S W
```

WORD SCRAMBLE

A good detective uses clues to solve a mystery. Can you complete the below sentence by unscrambling the ten clues?

When the Underdogs finally find Mick Wagger's golden guitar, his performance is going to be totally _ _ _ - _ _ _ _.

TMEPTRU	_ _ _ _ Ⓞ _ _
ITLLOECCNO	_ _ _ _ _ _ _ _ _
OIONADTN	_ _ _ Ⓞ _ _ _ _
RAOEWBRD	Ⓞ _ _ _ _ _ _ _
OASLRLRDLEBE	_ _ _ _ _ _ _ _ _ _ Ⓞ
OLHTE	_ Ⓞ _ _ _
EPTASMED	_ _ _ Ⓞ _ _ _ _
YLCUK	_ _ _ _ _
SETANOG	_ _ _ _ _ _ _
TCERCON	_ _ _ _ Ⓞ _ _

SPOT THE DIFFERENCE

A good detective knows when something is out of place. Can you find the ten differences between these two pictures?

ANSWER KEY

So how did you do?

```
I N G V K P A C J W H W J A E
G T Z M Q L C V J S F Z U X C
V I E M X O Z R Y W Z W X J N
O O U S S T Z Q N B S Q W P E
F P K T D L S T T K F R V T I
U U U U P A I W X E Z A G F D
L M A C K Y E M B Y F L M P U
E R A T I U G H O B T Y W N A
Z J O T B S I V M O Z L D P W
S P F W B A S D X A R Q E A O
N T C L I P B O A R D E K C U
Y X R A A H Q E U D H E R F X
V J N A L F R I L S X U D A D
F N M O Y A V J M P D B Y D J
W U G G O L D E N R O Q I S W
```

WORD SCRAMBLE

Trumpet, Collection, Donation, Wardrobe, Rollerblades, Hotel, Stampede, Lucky, Onstage, Concert

Answer to the clues:
Paw-some!

SPOT THE DIFFERENCE

THE UNDERDOGS ARE ON THE CASE!
DON'T MISS ANY OF THEIR ADVENTURES!